DILYS PRICE

NORMA
PRICE

BELLA
LASAGNE

JAMES

SARAH

MEET ALL THESE FRIENDS IN BUZZ BOOKS:

Thomas the Tank Engine
The Animals of Farthing Wood
Biker Mice From Mars
James Bond Junior
Fireman Sam
Joshua Jones
Rupert
Babar

First published in Great Britain by Buzz Books,
an imprint of Reed Children's Books
Michelin House, 81 Fulham Road, London SW3 6RB
and Auckland, Melbourne, Singapore and Toronto

Based on the animation series produced by Bumper Films
for S4C/Channel 4 Wales and Prism Art & Design Limited
Original idea by Dave Gingell and Dave Jones,
assisted by Mike Young. Characters created by Rob Lee.

ISBN 1 85591 386 0

Printed in Italy by Olivotto

NORMAN AND THE CLEVER BUDGIE

Story by Rob Lee
Illustrations by The County Studio

Norman Price was at Trevor's house to see his new budgie.

"His name's Busby," said Trevor.

"Who's a pretty boy?" squawked Busby.

"He's brill!" beamed Norman.

Norman and Trevor were so busy playing with Busby that they didn't notice Rosa the cat wandering in through the open door.

Suddenly, Rosa jumped onto the table for a closer look at the budgie. Busby squawked loudly and flew out of the open door!

Trevor tried to catch him, but Busby soared into the sky and out of sight.

"Oh no!" exclaimed Trevor.

"I'll get my skateboard and find him," said Norman, and he ran out of the door.

"You are a rascal," Trevor told Rosa.

Rosa miaowed.

At Pontypandy Fire Station, Firefighter Penny Morris was unloading the cutting equipment from Venus, the rescue tender.

"I'm representing Newtown Fire Brigade in the car-cutting competition," she told Fireman Sam. "The fastest firefighter to cut up the car wins. May I practise here?"

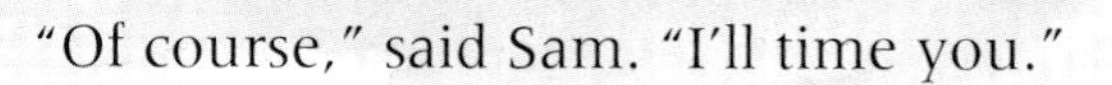

"Of course," said Sam. "I'll time you."

"Thanks," Penny replied. "The quicker I can cut up a car, the quicker I can rescue someone who might be trapped inside."

She set up her equipment next to the rusting shell of a car which sat in the corner of the station yard.

Just then, Station Officer Steele appeared.

"I've had a call from Trevor," he said. "Busby the budgie has flown away."

"We'll keep an eye out for him, sir," replied Fireman Sam.

Norman was already searching the countryside for Trevor's budgie.

"Busby!" he called. "Busby!"

"It's no use," he groaned, as he pushed off down the lane on his skateboard. "I must have skated miles!"

Suddenly, as Norman skated past a patch of waste ground near Morgan's Farm, he heard a squawk.

"Who's a pretty boy?" said a voice from the nearby junkyard.

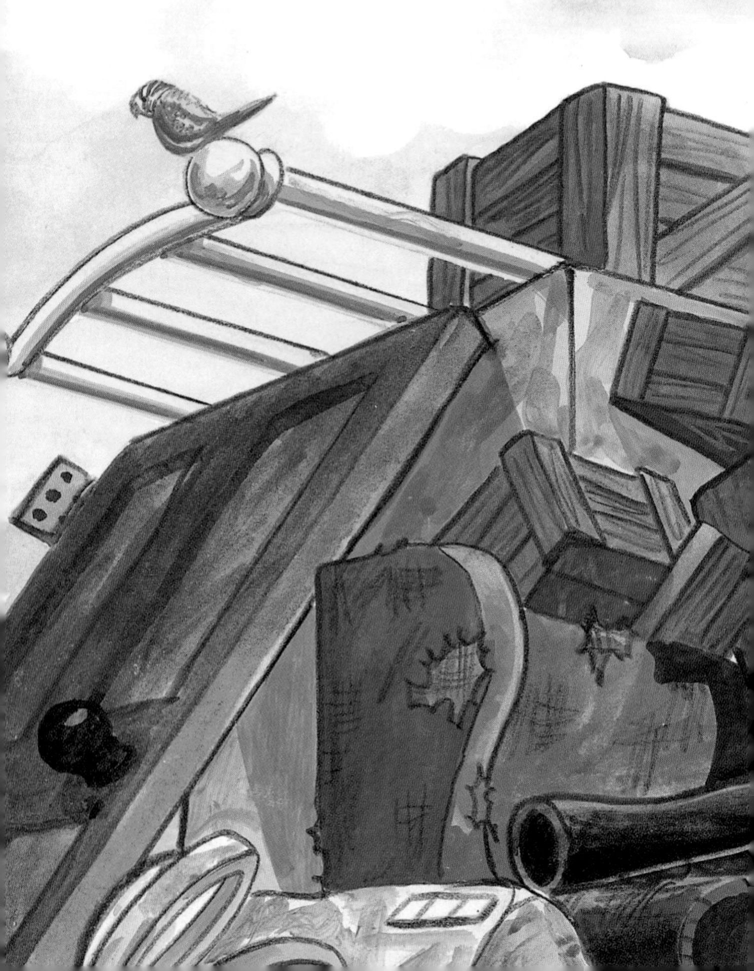

"That's Busby!" Norman exclaimed.

He grinned and skated towards the voice as quietly as he could. Perched on top of a pile of old pipes and broken furniture was Busby.

Quietly, Norman climbed up the scrap heap towards the budgie. He had nearly reached Busby, when suddenly, he slipped!

"Whoa!" he cried, as he tumbled down from the scrap heap, burying his skateboard under a pile of junk.

Alarmed by the noise, Busby took to the air with a squawk.

"Busby, come back!" called Norman.

He tried to follow the bird, but his leg was jammed beneath a pipe.

At the station, Penny had just finished cutting up the old banger.

"Not bad, Penny," said Sam, pressing the button on his stopwatch.

Just then, they heard a squawk. Fireman Sam gazed up at the station roof.

"Who's a pretty boy then?" said a cheeky bird.

"You must be Trevor's pet budgie!" exclaimed Sam.

But before he could make a move, Busby flew off again.

"Follow him!" cried Penny.

She and Sam jumped into the fire engine and raced after Busby. Sam kept track of the budgie, while Penny drove carefully.

Busby flew low in the sky, leading them to the countryside near Morgan's Farm.

"Stop here, Penny," said Sam, as Busby landed on a fence at the side of the lane.

As Sam and Penny crept towards Busby, a cry came from the scrap heap.

"Help! Help!"

"Great fires of London!" said Sam. "That sounds like Norman Price!"

They hurried across the waste ground to the scrap heap, where they found Norman sitting in the middle of a pile of junk.

"Are you okay, Norman?" asked Sam.

"I was trying to catch Busby," Norman replied. "But now my leg is trapped under this pipe."

"We can't lift the pipe because it's caught beneath the rest of the junk," said Penny. "This is a job for the cutting equipment."

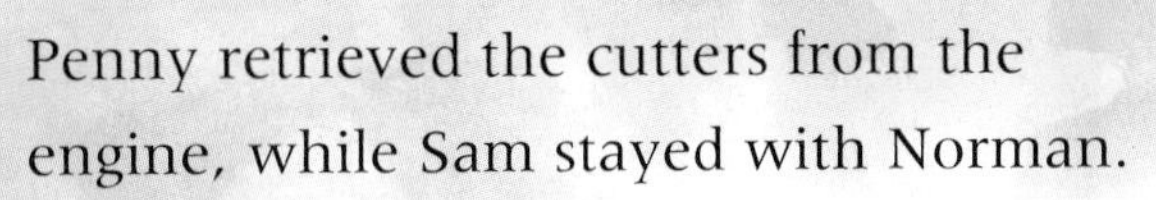

Penny retrieved the cutters from the engine, while Sam stayed with Norman.

"I'll have you free in a tick," Penny told Norman as she cut through the pipe.

Fireman Sam helped him to his feet.

"Well done, Penny," he said.

"Thanks, Penny," said Norman.

He rummaged through the junk that had scattered during his fall. At last, he found what he was looking for.

"Oh no!" he groaned, holding up his buckled skateboard.

Just then, Busby flew into sight and perched on Norman's shoulder.

"Who's a pretty boy?" Busby squawked.

"You are, Busby," chuckled Sam. "And a clever one, too, for leading us to Norman!"

Fireman Sam, Penny and Norman returned Busby to a delighted Trevor.

"I think he's had enough of life in the wild!" said Sam.

"Wants his tea, don't you, my beauty?" cooed Trevor.

Busby squawked loudly.

The next day, Penny treated Norman to an ice cream sundae at Bella's café.

"I won first prize in the car cutting competition," Penny told him. "And I'm sure that rescuing you from under that pipe gave me the extra practice I needed."

Trevor arrived, carrying a present for Norman — a brand new skateboard!

"This is to thank you for finding Busby for me," he said.

"Brill!" Norman exclaimed. "How did you know I'd broken my skateboard, Trevor?"

Trevor chuckled. "A little bird told me!"

FIREMAN SAM

STATION OFFICER
STEELE

TREVOR EVANS

ELVIS
CRIDLINGTON

PENNY MORRIS